To:

From:

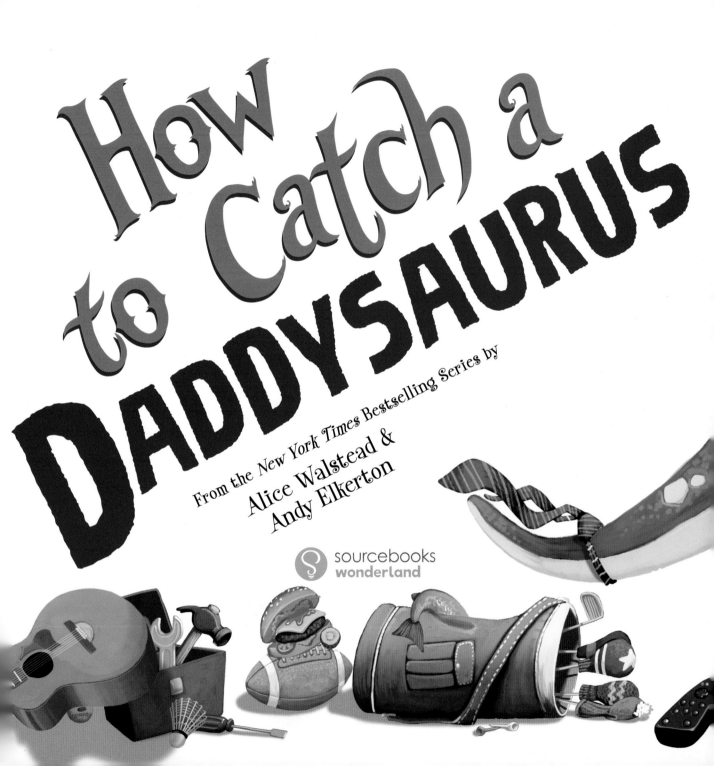

How to Catch a Daddysaurus

From the New York Times Bestselling Series by

Alice Walstead & Andy Elkerton

sourcebooks
wonderland

A legend is told of a creature near-perfect,
known for a **kindness** and bravery that's rare.
He's also loving, fun, patient, and smart—
to catch him will take a trap with great care.

He's busy for sure most of the time,
on the move from morning to night.
He does **everything** for his family,
making sure our days are all bright.

How does he do all that he does?
It must be **superpowers** no doubt.
Making sure we have whatever we need
with spare time to shake, twist, and shout!

This is it, the time has come!
Can't hold it back anymore.
Just love this **creature** so much.
Want to shout it with a big roar!

He says exercise is important.
Strong muscles are great, it's true.
It might be time for some **push-ups**–
these big weights are stuck like glue!

Daddysaurus has said more than once,
treat the things that we have with care.
He can **REPAIR** every room in the house—
don't think our skills here can compare.

If left up to us, we'd have a candy for **breakfast** then ice cream for lunch, it's true. But he doesn't let that happen. Sometimes we eat something he grew!

To be kind to others and share
are messages he makes sure we know.
And take the time to **appreciate** nature,
get outside and enjoy the sun's glow.

He's taught there are times to **WORK HARD**
and to get the job done, we know.
Just as there are times to play—
both are part of how we grow!

Sometimes he needs to correct us
when we stumble and do something wrong.
He makes clear he loves us no matter what.
His love is a **comfort** that's strong!

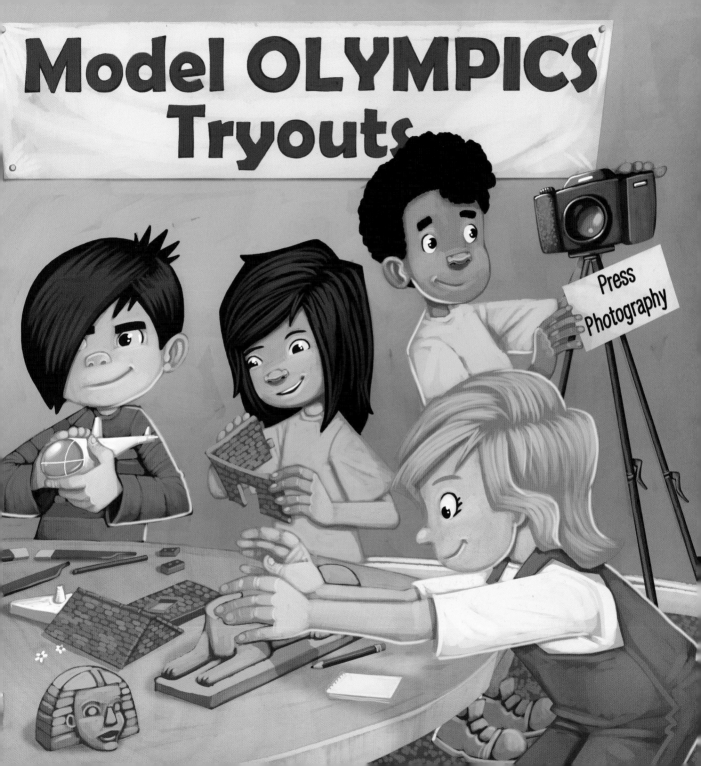

It's getting late, we're running out of time.
We're just bursting to share how we feel!
He's our lion, our coach, and our friend.
Because of him, we know **HEROES** are real.

How did we not see it before?
We've been going about this all WRONG.
We didn't need anything fancy–
the answer's been there all along!

To catch him, the trap is simple.
For how to set it, here is one clue.
All that we needed to say is:
DADDYSAURUS, we love you!

I LOVE YOU, DADDYSAURUS!

Write a note or draw your Daddysaurus!

Published by Sourcebooks Wonderland, an imprint of Sourcebooks Kids
P.O. Box 4410, Naperville, Illinois 60567–4410
(630) 961-3900
sourcebookskids.com

Cataloging-in-Publication Data is on file with the Library of Congress.

Source of Production: Wing King Tong, Shenzhen, Guangdong Province, China
Date of Production: October 2022
Run Number: 5027193

Printed and bound in China.
WKT 10 9 8 7 6 5 4 3 2 1

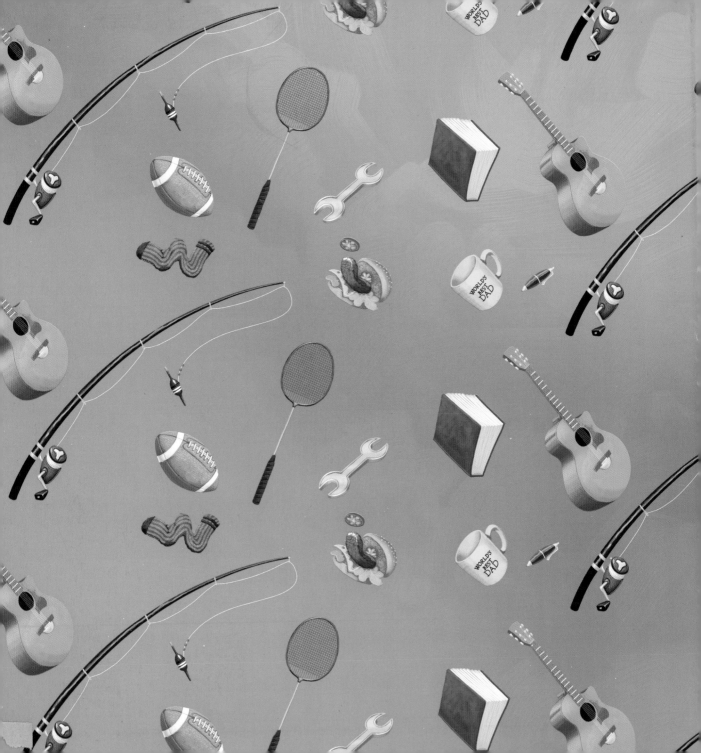